🔊 Listen and sing along to the song!
"Yellow Lotus Flower" By Jen Myzel

🟢 SPotify

🎵 iTunes

▶️ You TuBe

🔵 Bit.ly/yellowlotus

Music Copyright © 2019 by Jen Myzel
Illustrations Copyright © 2019 by Hillary Mendoza

Inquiries should be addressed to :
Music and General Book inquiries: jenmyzel@gmail.com
Illustration Inquiries: hill.mendoza@gmail.com

ISBN:978-0-578-41021-0
LCCN: 2018913425
Printed in USA

YELLOW LOTUS FLOWER

HOW One Lonesome Seed Rose UP from the MUCK

Written By Jen Myzel

Illustrated By Hillary Mendoza

May all Beings find the **courage** to rise up from the muck.

Yellow Lotus Flower,
like the sun you
rise UP from
the Darkness

When tears come your heart **grows stronger,** like the sun we rise UP from the Darkness

She asked the
Dragonflies
and the **frogs**
to sing along

Before she knew it there was a **Symphony** at the Pond

One lonesome yellow flower sharing her life song

I was Born at the
Bottom of this muck
A slimy seed I was
murky and stuck

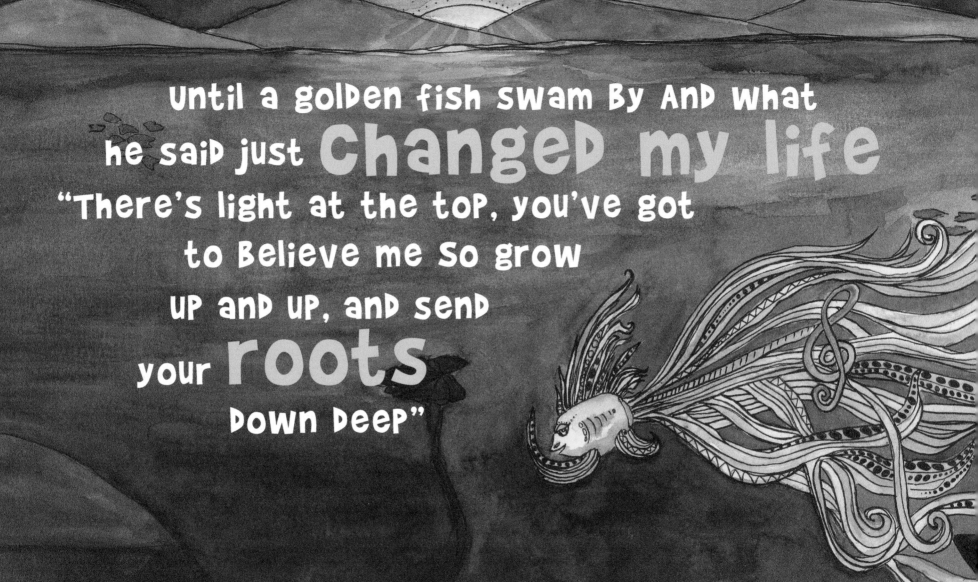

Until a golden fish swam by and what
he said just **changed my life**
"There's light at the top, you've got
to believe me so grow
up and up, and send
your **roots**

down deep"

Yellow Lotus Flower, like the sun you rise up from the Darkness

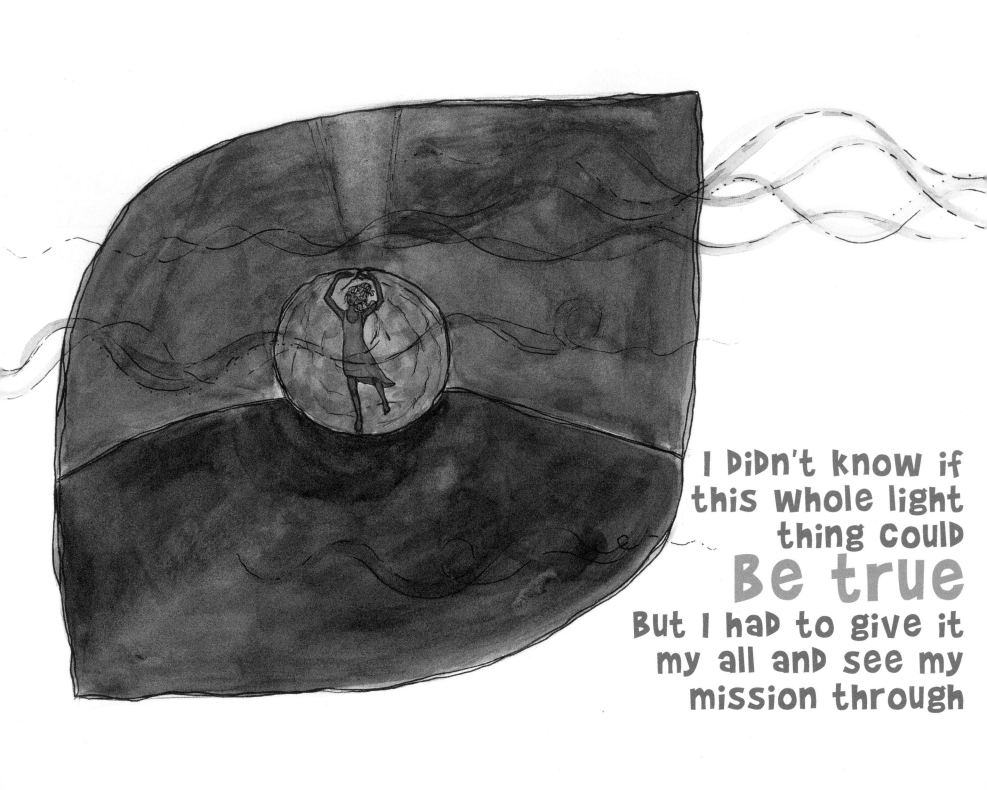

I Didn't know if this whole light thing could **Be true** But I had to give it my all and see my mission through

So I sent my roots down into the dark and watery Earth, It **CRACKED** my shell open and the Breaking was my Birth

My green arms were **growing,** my torso was getting strong

I could hear that golden fish, cheering me along

I tilted my body back and lifted my head up high

For the first time in my life, I felt the **Blue Beginning** of the sky

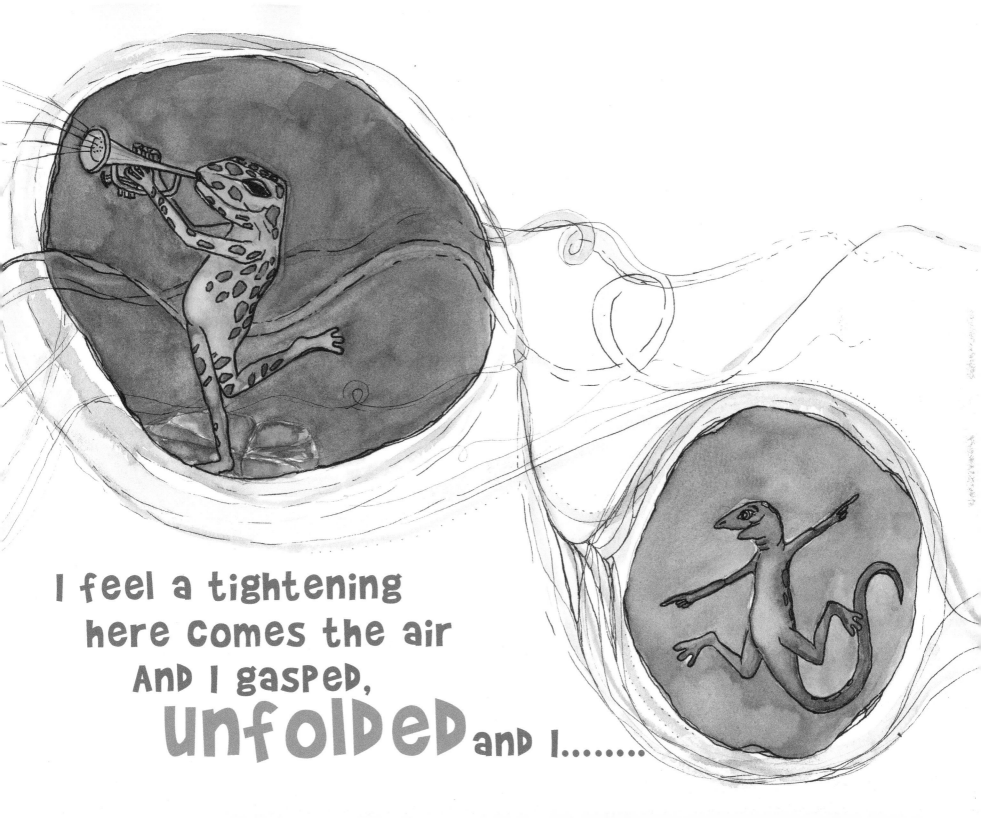

Opened my eyes, to the gracious sun and in that moment she looked back at me, we fell deeply in love

She warmed my yellow smile as I cried out loud I'd never felt so loved I didn't know I was allowed

The Sun said "Lotus Flower,
you are my sunshine
Oh won't you let my light in
for the rest of your life"

Yellow
Lotus
Flower,
like the sun you
rise up from
the Darkness

When tears come
your heart grows stronger,
like the sun we rise up
from the Darkness

Now that I'm all grown up
and shining like the sun
I like to sing my song for
each and every one

For the seeds
still in the mud,
and the buds who are on their way
FinD Courage
through the Dark,
and you will
Bloom one Day

Yellow Lotus Flower Guitar Chords

By Jen Myzel
Capo: 3rd fret

CHORUS

```
C       E       F           C
```
Yellow Lotus Flower, like the sun you rise up from the darkness
```
 C                              E             F
```
When tears come your heart grows stronger, like the sun we
```
 C
```
rise up from the darkness

VERSE 1

```
C       E       F           C
```
One yellow lotus flower wanted to sing a song
```
C          E           F          C
```
She asked the dragonflies and the frogs to sing along
```
C       E           F           C
```
Before she knew it there was a symphony at the pond
```
C       E       F           C
```
One lonesome yellow flower sharing her life song

BRIDGE 1

```
Am          G           F
```
I was born at the bottom of this muck
```
Am      G               F
```
A slimy seed I was murky and stuck

```
E           Am
```
Until a golden fish swam by
```
E               Am
```
And what he said just changed my life

```
        F                   C
```
There's light at the top, you've got to believe me
```
        F               C
```
So grow up and up, and send your roots down deep
```
C   E   F   C
```
Ooooooh Ooooooh

CHORUS

```
C       E           F           C           C E F C
```
Yellow Lotus Flower, like the sun you rise up from the darkness
```
 C                              E             F
```
When tears come your heart grows stronger, like the sun we
```
C           C E F C
```
rise up from the darkness

VERSE 2

```
C       E           F           C
```
I didn't know if this whole light thing could be true
```
C           E           F           C
```
But I had to give it my all and see my mission through
```
C           E           F           C
```
So I sent my roots down into the dark and watery Earth
```
C           E           F           C
```
It cracked my shell open and the breaking was my birth

INSTRUMENTAL
Am - E - F - C
Am - E - F - C

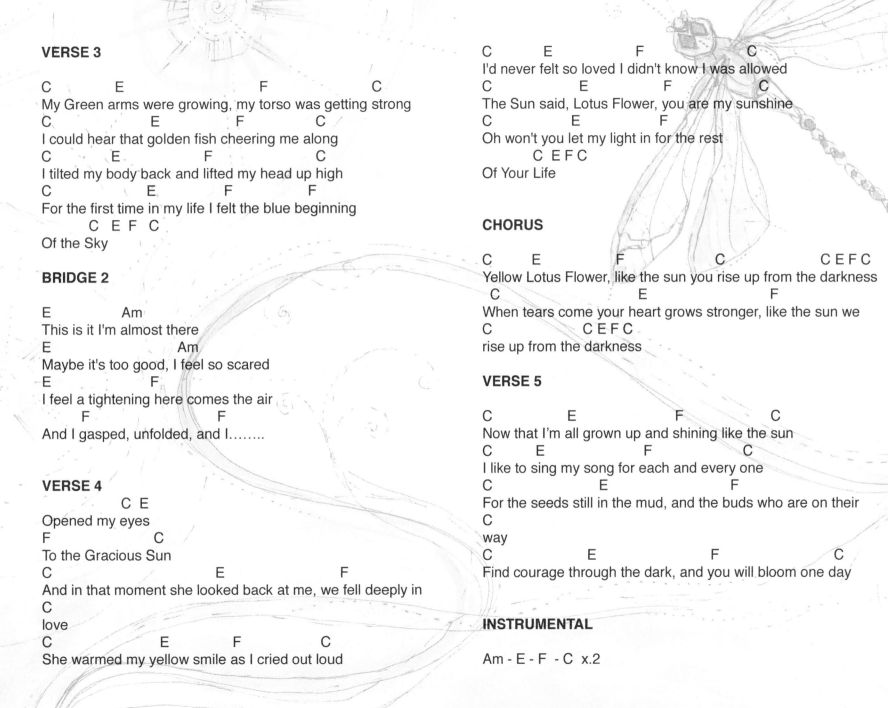

VERSE 3

```
C            E                    F            C
My Green arms were growing, my torso was getting strong
C            E              F           C
I could hear that golden fish cheering me along
C        E         F              C
I tilted my body back and lifted my head up high
C            E           F            F
For the first time in my life I felt the blue beginning
         C  E  F  C
Of the Sky
```

BRIDGE 2

```
E              Am
This is it I'm almost there
E                    Am
Maybe it's too good, I feel so scared
E               F
I feel a tightening here comes the air
         F              F
And I gasped, unfolded, and I........
```

VERSE 4

```
           C  E
Opened my eyes
F          C
To the Gracious Sun
C                           E              F
And in that moment she looked back at me, we fell deeply in
C
love
C          E         F          C
She warmed my yellow smile as I cried out loud
```

```
C            E              F            C
I'd never felt so loved I didn't know I was allowed
C            E              F            C
The Sun said, Lotus Flower, you are my sunshine
C            E              F
Oh won't you let my light in for the rest
            C E F C
Of Your Life
```

CHORUS

```
C        E          F             C          C E F C
Yellow Lotus Flower, like the sun you rise up from the darkness
         C                    E              F
When tears come your heart grows stronger, like the sun we
C              C E F C
rise up from the darkness
```

VERSE 5

```
C            E              F            C
Now that I'm all grown up and shining like the sun
C            E              F            C
I like to sing my song for each and every one
C            E              F
For the seeds still in the mud, and the buds who are on their
C
way
C            E              F            C
Find courage through the dark, and you will bloom one day
```

INSTRUMENTAL

```
Am - E - F - C x.2
```

ABout the Author and Illustrator:

Jen Myzel is a singer-songwriter and elementary school music teacher in Oakland, CA. Jen weaves personal and universal themes to create inspirational songs for children and adults. Hillary Mendoza is a multi-media artist, raw food chef and Ayurvedic practitioner in Northern California. The first time Hillary heard Jen's song "Yellow Lotus Flower", it brought her to tears. Those tears turned into watercolor paintings, and over the course of four years, their debut children's book, Yellow Lotus Flower, came to life.

For all inquiries regarding the music and book, contact: jenmyzel@gmail.com

For all inquiries regarding the illustrations, contact: hill.mendoza@gmail.com